Stinky Steve

A Minecraft Mishap

ISBN: 978-1536869101

# There's a free book waiting for you!

## Visit
www.montagepublishing.com/free-book-club

## MESSED-UP MINECRAFT

It's another great day in Minecraft.

Clouds float across the perfectly blue
sky as I go outside to check on my animals.
There was a small incident with the Creepers
last week so I'm happy to see that today the
chickens are safe and sound.

But what's going on with my pigs? Do they know something I don't? Their diet hasn't changed; are they sick? Afraid?

My body starts shaking - did someone install a new earthquake mod? That would certainly explain the animals' behavior. My body jerks forward; a loud explosion slams me into the fence. Like a wave of energy

hitting me from behind. Is someone

detonating TNT?

The pigs are still freaking out; there

must be a new threat in the area. I hope this

doesn't have anything to do with the pork chops I got in the village yesterday. (Pigs can be so sensitive.)

The pigs stare at me blankly, wrinkle their noses, then run to the other end of the pen.

As the pigs race away, I catch a whiff of something foul. (Pigs are not only sensitive; they're disgusting.)

I've lived in Minecraft for years, but I've never smelled anything like the stink that fills the air today – worse than a pile of zombies rotting in the sun.

I turn around to see what could possibly be fouling up this Minecraft universe.

There's a dark cloud hovering above the dirt, moving forward. Wait - it's following my every move. Oh no! Is that brown cloud coming out of ME?

## A CURIOUS PROBLEM

I run through my diet to see what could be causing this massive explosion of farts.

Wheat's never been a problem; I've been growing it for years. Cookies, bread, cake – always fine.

Same with pumpkins - I've baked pies

from day one with no incident at all.

Could this have anything to do with

that new bean mod that was added the

other day? I've always had cocoa beans but

the beans in this new mod were kidney,

pinto, navy, black, fava, white – nothing I've

ever encountered in Minecraft before.

Am I the only Steve with

uncontrollable farts or did other players

download the bean mod too? Is my perfect

Minecraft world on its way to being

destroyed – by me?

Without warning, another fart blasts

out of my backside. I feel a slight breeze and

realize I've blown a hole in the back of my

pants.

The chickens cover their faces with their wings while the pigs bury their heads in the mud. Is the smell THAT bad?

It is.

The chicken closest to me faints from the stench. I feel bad but there's still work to be done; the pigs and chickens will just have to put up with the smell.

I run inside and change my pants, then plant two rows of wheat, two rows of pumpkins, and two rows of corn.

Chickens dive into the dirt and several pigs run in circles, trying to outrun the brown cloud following them.

I'm not thrilled with the prospect of being alone in the house all night with this smell, but hopefully I worked hard enough today that I'll fall right to sleep.

## UNWANTED GUESTS

In bed, I feel like I'm choking from the

smell.  I stick my head under my red blanket

but that doesn't help. Not even my awesome

inventory can assist me today.

I open a book and cover my face with it. No luck. I hide inside my chest but that doesn't help either. Finally, I smash holes into the window to get some fresh air. Too bad if the pigs and chickens complain - I need to breathe!

There's rustling outside – I knew the chickens and pigs would make a fuss once I 'opened' the window.  But when I look out, it's not the animals I hear but Creepers.

I'm going to scare these Creepers away with this new ammunition coming out of my butt. I head to the yard and get ready

to blast one out.

Yes! A direct hit!

But instead of running away, the

Creepers are ATTRACTED by the smell. At

first there were three or four but suddenly

there are dozens, coming from every

direction.

The Creepers trip over themselves to reach me. The pigs and chickens go crazy, running around the enclosures in a panic.

The mobs chase me around the house and for the first time, I think it may collapse. The Creepers are hissing even louder than normal. What do I do now?

Open my inventory, that's what.

I rummage through my chest to find the most appropriate weapon. Iron sword?

Pickaxe?

I grab the sword to fend off these pesky Creepers; fortunately, the smell keeps them from exploding when they get too close. In a break in the battle, I access my inventory.

Shield?

Rope?

Then I see the TNT.

I grab the shovel and head outside. It's as if each fart spawns a new horde of Creepers.

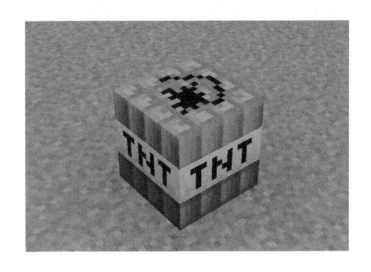

## WHY CAN'T I STOP FARTING?

I dig a hole underneath my house, making sure I'm at least eight blocks away from the foundation so I don't blow up my Minecraft home. I place the explosive blocks near the surface and blow up the Creepers by detonating the TNT with flint and steel, making sure I'm far enough away so they don't explode too close to me.

The plan worked – I destroyed most of them and scared the rest away!

After they're gone, I calm down the animals. Tonight was a narrow escape; I've got to get this farting under control.

Once I harvest the new crops tomorrow, I'll be all set. My flatulence problem will be officially solved. I hope.

## BEANS, BEANS, THE MAGICAL FRUIT

The next morning, the only sign of Creepers is the giant hole in the yard. It's time to start my daily chores.

Feed animals – check.

Water the garden – check.

Harvest crops – check.

But instead of wheat, pumpkin, and corn, all the crops I planted have been replaced with more beans.

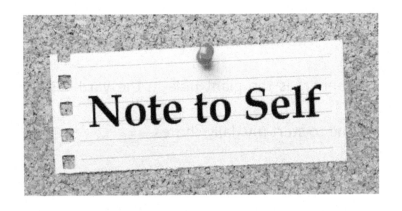

Note to self: always read the fine print when installing mods. I never would've installed that modification if I'd known the

beans would take over all my crops.

I harvest the beans - every kind

imaginable, in all shapes and sizes. (My butt

hurts just thinking about it.)

I know beans are the LAST thing I

should be eating right now, but last night's

Creeper attack took a lot of energy and I'm STARVING.  Would it be asking for trouble to eat more?

Against my better judgment, I chow down on a big bowl of beans.

I COULD go to the village and buy some normal food but my inventory's down.

There's only one thing left to do – see if any villagers will exchange other foods for beans. (At this point, I'll even eat a pufferfish.)

All I have to do is not fart in front of the villagers and I'll be fine.

## TRADING TROUBLE

Squeezing my butt cheeks together as tightly as I can, I enter the village. A farmer and librarian give me the evil eye - or should I say Stink Eye. I pass several villagers but I'm the only one trailing a brown cloud. (So much for controlling my butt.)

The villager who usually helps me doesn't grunt this time but fans himself and runs out of the store.

(It was definitely a mistake having more beans this morning.)

When I see the black apron villager, I get an idea. He can make me some iron leggings to contain my farts! But I don't have any emeralds to trade for them; I wonder if he'll take beans.

News spreads fast because when I get there, the black apron villager stuffs a helmet with wool to create a gas mask to block my stink. It's a good thing because he's my only hope. I think about asking him for a chest plate and helmet too, but he tosses me out of the store, eager to get rid of me. I slip

on the iron leggings – they're perfect! Just

what I need to contain these stinky farts.

I hear a roar in my stomach, and the

next sound I hear is the screeching sound of

metal being torn apart.

My farts have blown out my iron leggings!

This is terrible!

Living in Minecraft, I've always dealt with mobs: Creepers, zombies, skeletons, silverfish, even blazes in the Nether, but I've never seen a mob as angry and violent as this one.

I guess passing the gas is enough to turn even the most neutral villager hostile. (Fishermen and farmers, sure. But priests, librarians, and children in an angry mob? Who knew?)

The priest waves his arms trying to exorcise the farts from my body while the farmer weeps at the sight of his wilted crops.

The villagers grunt and throw things. I race through the village chased by this new hostile mob, led by the black apron guy.

The beans weren't even that good! (Mushy and kind of bland.)

A few villagers fall by the wayside after I blast out a big one, but most of them cover their noses and wipe tears from their eyes as they chase me out of town.

Heading toward the water, I spot a small brown square. Is that a boat? I can't remember the last time I got into a boat, but now's not the time to be nostalgic.

I climb in and shove off into the stream, leaving the angry villagers behind in a cloud of brown smoke.

Goodbye, cruel world!

## ON THE RUN

I glance back at the villagers who are still throwing their inventory at me. Are my farts bad enough to lose your inventory over? I don't think so.

I duck as an apple whizzes by my head - a smarter Minecraft player might have caught it to eat later.

It's hard not to notice that every plant I pass shrivels into the soil. Sorry about that, guys!

I've logged a lot of time here but I'm

not familiar with this part of the river.

I look through my inventory at the

beans I'd planned on trading in the village –

TONS of them. All I want is some pumpkin

pie, some pork chops – anything but beans.

But they're all I have and I'm famished after

running from that angry mob of villagers and

I have no choice but to eat several handfuls.

Drifting along, the terrain changes and I realize I'm heading toward a swamp biome. I can't remember the last time I was in one; it's actually kind of relaxing. The trees are covered with vines, some of them surrounded by clumps of mushrooms.

If I remember correctly, chickens spawn here and sure enough, a few chickens appear onshore. The trees, however, are dark, and I'd be lying if I said I wasn't scared.

Have I been banished to the swamp to live out the rest of my days as a hermit in a boat with only my farts to keep me company?

Wait! There's something off in the distance.

Is that a witch's hut?

## WITCH WATCH

I've seen witches a few times in Minecraft but not as much as Creepers or zombies. I tiptoe toward the hut, trying to keep quiet, although the witches would probably smell me first.

Inside are a cauldron and a crafting table that someone must've left behind. I

can make a potion to get me out of this

farting mess!

I look through all the potions already

there - potions of fire resistance, swiftness,

water breathing - but nothing that looks like

it might help with my bean problem. If there

were a healing potion here, maybe that

would work, but I'm not sure any of these

will do the trick. I guess I can use one of the

glass bottles to brew my own potion – but

what ingredients should I use?

I rummage through the rest of the hut

and find a beaker of Night Vision potion

and a brewing stand. Now we're talking! I

can make an invisibility potion! Then I can

finally get back home.

I carefully take out the brewing stand and put the Night Vision potion in one of the bottom boxes in the menu. I go through my inventory, grab the fermented spider eye, and add it to the top box. (I KNEW that would come in handy someday.) I wait impatiently for the fermented spider eye to disappear – when it does, the potion is ready.

I drink the potion down and hope for the best.

It worked! I'm now invisible! This is amazing!

But wait – I still smell!

My body may no longer be visible, but the brown cloud behind me certainly is. What am I going to do?

I'd better come up with something fast, because there are noises outside.

The witches are back.

## TOOT TROUBLE

Even though I'm invisible, I still have to hide because of the toxic cloud. I duck behind the large table but the brown cloud behind me gives me away.

One witch douses me with a potion of weakness, which immediately makes me visible again. Another witch raises her hand to stop the others. I watch them from behind the table and wonder what they're talking about.

As they discuss the intruder - me - I realize none of them are complaining about the smell. They definitely SEE the brown cloud, but they appear to be immune to the odor. Maybe they'll just let me go in peace.

The first witch smiles. This is great —

I'm happy to be on my way. But the witches

have no intention of letting me go. It takes a

moment for me to realize why.

They want to capture the farts for themselves!

I make a run for it but as I head toward the boat, a witch in back throws a potion of slowness and I'm suddenly running at the pace of a snail.

Before I know it, the witches descend

on me with their empty potion bottles. I

pinch my butt cheeks together to hopefully

foil their plan. (Foil, not soil.)

But the witches are on a fart mission

and can't be stopped.

I realize I now have a NEW problem –

it's a full moon and I'm in a swamp.

Right on cue, my worst fears are realized.

Here comes the slime.

## SLIME VS. WITCHES

Now I have to fight TWO mobs? This is completely and totally unfair! And all because I ate some beans? (Okay, a LOT of beans, but still...)

The witches are obsessed with filling their potion bottles while the slime come at me from all angles.  Some swim, some hop,

some get in the way of the witches.


A small fight breaks out near the hut;

the witches seem pretty territorial about this

corner of the biome.  (Fighting over who can

get closer to the person farting is definitely

something new.)

The ruckus gets larger and louder so I use the opportunity to climb up one of the trees to hide.

From the canopy of trees, I have a great view of the action.

Will I be able to make it to the boat without anyone seeing me? Should I figure out a way to farm the mobs or make slime balls out of them? And why do the witches want to bottle my farts so badly? Do they know something I don't? They obviously think my flatulence is a GOOD thing – maybe I've been looking at this problem all wrong. Maybe I'M the one with the power in this situation.

Instead of escaping like a coward, I decide to test my newfound power. Grabbing the nearest vine, I swing above the brawling crowd and let one rip.

I crop dust from one end of the swamp to the other, leaving the witches and slime in a cloud of stink.

Limbs fly up to grab me as I swing across the swamp on the vine, finishing off by landing expertly inside the boat. I stick my butt in the water and create the first

outboard motor fueled by farts.

It takes the mobs a few minutes to

realize I'm gone and by the time they do, I'm

already upriver.

As I steer the boat toward home, I decide to make the most of my new bean power. Minecraft NEEDS a superhero – why can't it be me? STINKY STEVE TO THE RESCUE – it's got a nice ring to it.

The gods above must also think it's a good idea because thunder suddenly erupts, filling the valley with its deafening roar.

My bad. It was just another fart.


STINKY STEVE TO THE RESCUE!

## EPILOGUE

*Does Steve actually think I'm going to*

*let him get away with becoming a Superhero?*

*Flying through these perfectly blue skies*

*solving crime? Minecraft is MY terrain, not*

*his. He has no idea who he's up against.*

The villain watches Steve float lazily

downriver toward his home. It would be easy

to attack from above or below — Steve

certainly wouldn't expect anything now. The villain heads to the chest in the corner of the room to prepare.

Splash potion of harming?

Diamond Sword?

Tipped Arrow?

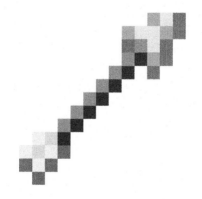

Or perhaps waiting is a better idea. Maybe setting a trap for this new "Superhero" will be more effective than just conquering him now. It certainly would be more fun. And isn't that what it's all about?

Steve obviously thinks the Minecraft universe is on his side – how very wrong he is.

The villain sits in front of the furnace to think. Is it best to fight this farting superhero alone or should a few colleagues be enlisted?

Creepers?

Zombies?

No...watching Steve battle Spider Jockeys will be much more entertaining.

*This is going to be fun!*

# There's a free book waiting for you!

## Visit:
www.montagepublishing.com/free-book-club

# Leave Me A Review

Please support me by leaving a review.
The more reviews I get,
the more books I will write!

"It's Pooptastic!"

## Connect with PT Evans

Twitter: @PTEvansAuthor
Instagram: @PTEvansAuthor
Facebook: facebook.com/PTEvansAuthor

# INTRODUCING STINKY STEVE!!

BOOK ONE: A Minecraft Mishap
BOOK TWO: Minecraft Superhero

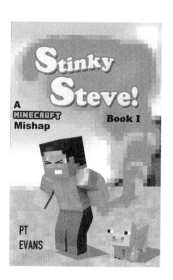

# Also by PT Evans

## App Mash-up!

### Volume 1
### Minecraft vs Angry Birds

### Volume 2
### Fruit Ninja and Candy Crush
(coming soon)

# More by PT Evans

## MINECAT: A Feline Minecraft™ Adventure

BOOK ONE: A Whole Lot Of Ocelots
BOOK TWO: Sugar Cane Rush

# Ready for an Emoji Adventure?

# Make A Cameo

Want to be a Character in the next Emoji Adventures
Book?
Enter at:
www.EmojiAdventuresBook.com

## MONTAGE PUBLISHING

**Connect with Montage Publishing**

Twitter: @MontageBooks
Instagram: @MontagePublishing
Facebook: facebook.com/montagepublishing
www.MontagePublishing.com

Made in the USA
Coppell, TX
11 October 2020